P9-CQQ-818

In memory of Mother
          —P. H.

For Alana
          —G. B. K.

A Bill Martin Book
Henry Holt and Company   New York

My Crayons Talk

PATRICIA HUBBARD

illustrations by

G. BRIAN KARAS

Talk. Talk.
My crayons talk.
Yackity. Clackity.
Talk. Talk. Talk.

Purple shouts, "Yum!
Bubble gum."

Brown sings, "Play,
Mud-pie day."

Blue calls, "Sky,
Swing so high."

Yellow chirps, "Quick,
Baby chick."

Talk. Talk.
My crayons talk.
Yackity. Clackity.
Talk. Talk. Talk.

Gold brags, "Fine,
Dress up time."

Silver toots, "Grand,
Marching band."

Red roars, "No,
Do not go."

Green yells, "Fun!
Watch me run."

Talk. Talk.
My crayons talk.
Yackity. Clackity.
Talk. Talk. Talk.

Orange asks, "Sweet,
May I eat?"

Black hoots, "Wise,
Big owl eyes."

White screams, "Most
Scary ghost."

Pink laughs, "Clown! Pants fall down!"

Talk. Talk.
My crayons talk.
Yack yack yackity.
Chit chat clackity.
Yackity. Clackity.
Talk. Talk. Talk.

Bill Martin Jr, Ph.D., (1916–2004) devoted his life to the education of young children. Bill Martin Books reflect his philosophy: that children's imaginations are opened up through the play of language, the imagery of illustration, and the permanent joy of reading books.

Henry Holt and Company, LLC, *Publishers since 1866*
175 Fifth Avenue, New York, New York 10010
www.HenryHoltKids.com

Henry Holt® is a registered trademark of Henry Holt and Company, LLC.
Text copyright © 1996 by Patricia Hubbard
Illustrations copyright © 1996 by G. Brian Karas
All rights reserved. Distributed in Canada by H. B. Fenn and Company Ltd.

Library of Congress Cataloging-in-Publication Data
Hubbard, Patricia.
My crayons talk / by Patricia Hubbard; illustrations by G. Brian Karas
"A Bill Martin Book"
Summary: Brown crayon sings "Play, Mud-pie day," and Blue crayon calls
"Sky, Swing so high" in this story about talking crayons.   [1. Color—Fiction.
2. Crayons—Fiction. 3. Stories in rhyme.]   I. Karas, G. Brian, ill. II. Title.
PZ8.3.H8475My 1995 [E]—dc20 95-12786

ISBN 978-0-8050-3529-2 (hardcover)
20 19 18 17 16 15 14 13 12 11 10 9
ISBN 978-0-8050-6150-5 (paperback)
20 19 18

First published in hardcover in 1996 by Henry Holt and Company
First paperback edition—1999
The artist used crayons, gouache, acrylic, and pencil on Strathmore bristol board
to create the illustrations for this book.
Printed in December 2010 in China by South China Printing Company Ltd., Dongguan City,
Guangdong Province

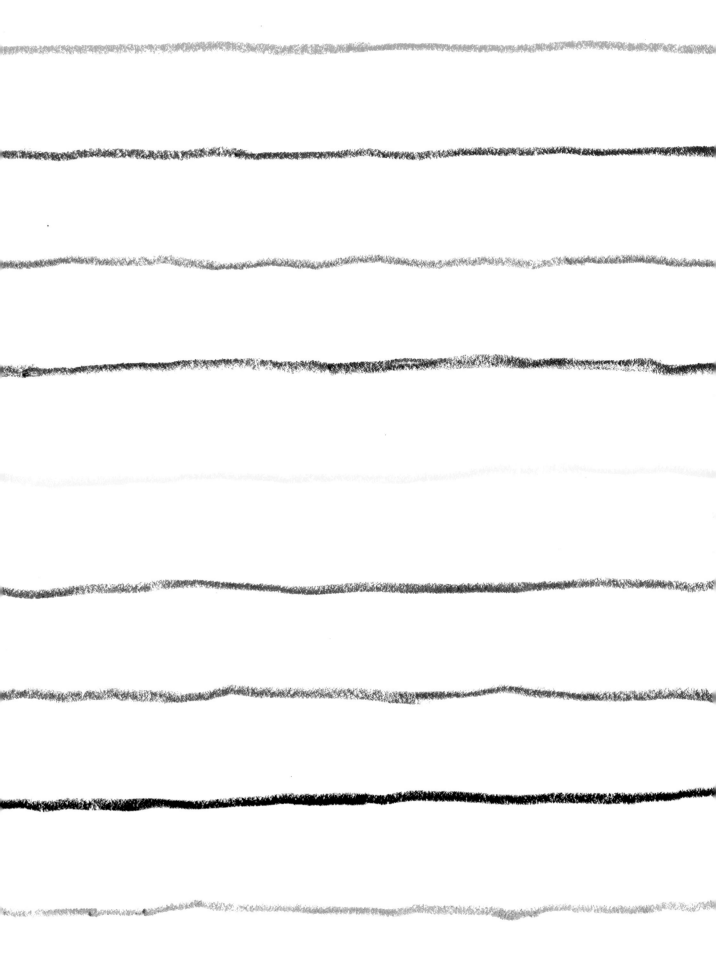